Jade

Remember, mystery and adventure can sometimes be found in the most unusual of places!

Jocelyn x

Chapter 1

Have you ever felt every emotion all in one swirl like an enormous Mr Whippy? Happy, nervous, worried, anxious, excited... well that's how Jade felt as she stared at herself in the mirror in her new school uniform. It was a bit on the big side but her Mum said she could grow into it, her Mum also said she looked smart. The clothes felt unfamiliar and the blazer was a little bit itchy. Jade adjusted her tie and took a deep breath...

'Ok, let's do this' she said to her reflection.

Rocksway Secondary School was a pretty normal secondary school; you know the type, big grey building with lots of windows, desks, chairs etc. It was the beginning of the new school year and one of the many New Year 7s was Jade, and she was by far the most nervous, or at least this is what she thought. Jade is average height with tanned skin the colour of melted milk chocolate and almost as smooth. She has bright green eyes and long dark hair that falls to her waist.

It was a bright September morning, but Jade wasn't feeling bright she was feeling glum as she trudged her way to school dreading the thought of not having any friends. Having been home schooled since she was four meant that she didn't really know what school was going to be like and she knew sure as the sun would set that she wouldn't know any other children.

Jade reached the school gates, took a deep breath and started to weave her way through the crowds of children. She smiled shyly at the new faces some smiled back but others turned away. A group of older girls stood giggling over a picture on their phones, they didn't even notice as Jade slipped past them, others stood around chatting and seeming completely at ease. Jade felt awkward and a little lost. The first thing she needed to do was get her locker key, that's what the letter had said that her mum had received, she checked on the note in her pocket 'locker 50' that's what was allocated to her. Jade headed into the building to where a teacher was giving out the keys and directing pupils to their lockers.

Jade waited patiently in line, the queue moved quicker than she thought it would, and soon it was her turn.

'Good morning, what number locker do you have?' asked the teacher Jade thought she must have asked the same question about 100 times that morning already, but she still smiled broadly, the teacher seemed very caring and warm, her name badge read Miss Burton.

'Good morning, number 50, please!' replied Jade.

The teacher looked surprised. 'Are you sure?' she asked Jade peering over her glasses 'we've not used that locker for years'.

'Oh....ermmm.... Yes Miss Burton I had a letter, it definitely said locker 50' Jade replied shyly.

The teacher stilled puzzled turned to her tray of keys and searched through the compartments, it seemed to take her a while and Jade was worried that a big queue was building up behind her.

'Ah... here we are' Miss Burton exclaimed eventually 'It must have been hiding!' She handed Jade a small gold key on a keyring that simply had a large number 50 on the tag.

Jade popped the key in her pocket and listened carefully to the directions, which did seem quite complicated, but she didn't want to ask twice as she was embarrassed to hold the queue up any longer.

Jade made her way down the first corridor, she pushed through some double doors and past children that were already filling their lockers with PE kits and books, they were chatting about their summer holidays, 'They must have been in the same primary school together' Jade thought, feeling jealous that they already had good friends. Moving on Jade took a right down a smaller corridor that was less busy, this is when she bumped into a girl.

'Oh gosh I'm sorry' said Jade.

'Hey that's ok' the girl smiled back, this is when Jade noticed she had the same unusually bright green eyes just like hers.

'My names Em' she said.

Em was petite in stature with an even sprinkling of freckles across her nose and cheeks. She had almost white blonde short hair and a big smile that stretched across her face creating dimples in her rosy cheeks . She looked easy going as if nothing much would phase her.

'I'm Jade, nice to meet you' they smiled at each other 'I was just looking for my locker have you found yours?' Jade asked.

Em replied in an instant 'Yes its just down the corridor from here, I was just heading to the hall for the first assembly thingy-a-me -jig !' Em giggled.

'Goodness, is it time for that already, I must have spent way too long looking for my locker' Jade said checking her watch. 'And I've completely forgotten about picking my timetable from the reception', Jade groaned looking worried. There seemed to be so much to think about and remember, how was she ever going to manage?

' Well' Em said looking concerned 'what set are you in?'

'7ZL' Jade replied.

'No way! Me too, that sorts the timetable problem, you can use mine for today' replied Em.

'Thank you that's very kind; well if we get lost then at least we'll get lost together, this place seems so huge' Jade said.

The girls made their way to the hall together, as they went they chatted happily just like they had been friends for a very long time. Em explained she was worried as she didn't know anyone as her parents had recently moved to the area, and Jade told her about being nervous as she too didn't know anyone due to being home schooled. The girls laughed at the coincidence and spontaneously hugged giving each other reassurance that neither would now be alone.

The assembly hall was in the newer part of the school and it was light and bright, there was a stage at one end and what seemed like hundreds of black plastic chairs in rows, the girls filed in with all the other Year 7s and took a seat. The Head Teacher spoke enthusiastically about the school and told them all to make the most of their school days at Rocksway, Jade sat and listened quietly, she did still feel rather nervous and overwhelmed, but glancing across to Em she felt happy and relieved that she'd at least made a friend.

Chapter 2

The first lesson was English. Jade and Em used the school map to locate Mr March's English classroom it was situated in the older part of the school. Mr March stood in the doorway watching the new pupils walk in. He was a tall and imposing person. He had jet black hair scattered with grey and it was gelled back from his unkind face, his eyes were the darkest shade of brown Jade had ever seen.

'Good morning, take a seat' he said in a stern manner.

Although Mr March was smiling the smile looked fake, it looked like he wasn't used to smiling and it was a real effort, Jade remembered the welcoming, kind smile of Miss Burton, and this was very much the opposite.

As Jade and Em found their seats, Mr March was watching them intently as if something was bothering him.

The lesson was a little dull and English droned on for what felt like hours, all the while Jade couldn't help but think that Mr March had taken a dislike to her and

Em, the way he kept staring at them made her feel very uncomfortable, it was as though they were doing something wrong.

Jade's mind started to wander and she thought to herself, 'through the excitement of meeting Em, I never actually opened my locker', the small gold key was in her blazer pocket.

She snapped back to reality as Mr March called her name, not sure what to say (as she hadn't been listening) she opted for 'Yes, Sir'.

Mr March glared at Jade 'This is NOT the register, I was asking you what a pronoun is' he ranted. 'I'm giving you a lunch time detention for not paying attention' he looked strangely pleased with himself. Jade was flabbergasted, a detention on her first day, just great.

On the way to lunch Em told her she'd heard that in detention you get your fingers pulled one by one until you cried; which Jade knew couldn't possibly be true.

'Wasn't it strange how Mr March kept staring at us as if we had done something wrong?' Jade said.

'Well you kinda did, remember....daydreamer' Em said jokingly.

'But did you see the look he gave us when we walked in? It was weird like he was surprised and cross all in one; I almost sensed he didn't want us to be there' Jade explained.

'Maybe that's just how he is, I'm sure he just sees us as a couple of pesky students' Em laughed.

Jade didn't have long to eat her lunch and was still finishing off her apple as she made her way to Mr March's office. She knocked on his door and waited but he didn't answer, she knocked again a little more firmly, still no answer. The door was slightly ajar so she peeped through the gap: the office was quite small and very tidy, it was mostly taken up by a large desk and an equally large black leather chair. There was also a filing cabinet and a second much smaller desk and chair situated under the window. On the windowsill were some rather dead looking plants, even from where Jade stood she could see they were covered in dust and cobwebs.

'Mr March?' she called, just then a door to the back of the office opened and Mr March strode out holding some paperwork, he caught sight of Jade, hurriedly folded what he was carrying in two, and shut the door behind him with force.

'Don't you knock?' questioned Mr March, Jade didn't think it would be sensible to say she had as Mr March seemed cross enough with her already.

'Sorry Sir.'

'Well come in then', he almost growled.

Jade picked up her bag and pushed the door fully open 'Sir, I'm very sorry for not paying attention I....'

But before she could finish her sentence Mr March interrupted her 'Well you know why you're here, do you have a pen and paper?'

'Yes Sir' Jade said reaching in her bag.

'Ok, take a seat' Mr March pointed to the table under the dusty windowsill 'I want you to write me a paragraph on why we should pay attention in class.'

Jade started her writing, keeping her head down she only dared to glance up a couple of times. Mr March seem to be studying the papers that he got from his storage room, he was smirking and seemed pleased with what he was looking at. Jade turned her attention back to the paragraph, satisfied she had finished the task properly, she put her pen down 'Excuse Mr March, I've finished the paragraph.'

Mr March again folded the papers he had been studying in two, and held out his hand.

'Bring it to me'

Jade stood and waited as he scanned through her work 'Hummm, ok' he said and in very scrawly handwriting wrote ' *Detention completed* '

'Now collect up your things and go to your next lesson' he instructed.

Just at that moment the dust from the plants on the window sill must have tickled Jades nose and she let out an almighty sneeze, 'Bless me' she said. As she pulled a tissue out of her blazer pocket her locker key tumbled to the floor. Mr March froze, Jade thought he was mad with her for sneezing (after all it was a very loud sneeze!) but then she noticed he was just staring at her locker key on the floor.

'Number 50?' he almost spat the words out.

'Yes, Sir' Jade picked up the key and wiped her nose on the tissue.

'That can't be right, who gave you that locker?' he demanded.

'Miss Burton' Jade replied confused as to why Mr March was worrying about her locker.

'I shall double check this with Miss Burton...I'll do it right away....Ok you can go now' Mr March was looking worried and cross and clearly wanted Jade gone. Jade didn't want to hang around either and hurriedly picked up her pen and her bag, not wanting to stay any longer than necessary.

'Well that was odd' Jade thought, she'd have to report the whole thing back to Em, whilst it turned out not to be a pleasant experience at least there was no finger pulling!

Meanwhile, at the same time on the other side of the school, Marblo the cleaner was sweeping the hallway when he heard a strange cawing sound coming from somewhere, he scratched his head in puzzlement as it seemed to be coming from the wall or at least the locker block, and it certainly sounded like a macaws call! 'Very strange' he thought I've not heard a noise like that in years. Then a worried look came over his normally happy face.

Chapter 3

Over breakfast the following morning Jade wrote LOCKER on her hand to remind her to go to her locker. With all the happenings on the first day she never actually made it there.

'Is everything OK sweetheart?' her mum asked 'You seem a little quiet.'

'Everything's fine, yesterday was a very exciting day, I guess I'm still a little tired' She smiled up at her mum.

'Ok, good, I was worried you didn't enjoy your first day at school....I know it's going to be strange but I'm sure you'll get the hang of it all.'

'Yes, it's certainly a little strange!' Jade agreed thoughtfully.

'Right, I must be off to work,' Jade's mum said popping the last bit of toast in her mouth and grabbing her hand bag 'Have a great day, and I'll see you later' She blew Jade a kiss as she headed out the door.

At school Jade tried to remember Miss Burton's directions from yesterday, Jade and Em rushed through the corridors in a desperate search for the locker before the bell went.

CRASH!! Jade skidded right into a cleaning bucket and mop which was sent flying. The owner of the bucket and mop hurried around the corner.

'I'm ever so sorry sir' Jade said whilst crossing her fingers that she wouldn't get another detention.

'No harm done' said the cleaner picking up the mop 'it's lucky the bucket was near enough empty, it was just an accident, partly my fault too, I shouldn't have left it just sat there' He smiled kindly '...and please call me Marblo, Sir just sounds too posh' he said chuckling.

Here's some information about Marblo; he was born in Jamaica but as a young boy he was thrown onto the streets because he had bright green eyes, but he also had a bright mind and made sure he went to the local school. It was at this school he met a kindly British teacher and she took him under her wing and when it was her time to return to England she took Marblo with her, he finished off his school days at Rocksway Secondary School. He grew up into a kind and considerate person who was always willing to help. After leaving school he worked as a gardener in the large tropical arboretum, people used to visit the place from miles away as the plants he looked after were the most beautiful they had ever seen. As he got older he returned to Rocksway and worked as the handy man and cleaner. He enjoyed his work and took pride in how the school looked; he also enjoyed the long holidays as it gave him enough time to turn his attention to his hobby which was growing exotic plants.

Jade asked Marblo if he knew where her locker was, and of course he did, he'd been working at the school for many years. He seemed very happy that she had locker 50, Jade was relieved someone seemed pleased after the reaction of Mr March she was thinking that locker 50 was an unlucky locker.

'You are the perfect person to look after that locker I can just tell, are you two best friends?' Marblo said in his warm Jamaican accent, waving his had from Jade to Em.

'Yes' the girls giggled, Marblo had such a funny manner, but so likeable.

'Perfect, that's just even better in fact' Marblo chuckled.

'Well I was cleaning outside locker 50 just yesterday' he said ' A strange thing happened' The girls leaned in as his voiced dropped to a whisper. At that moment a teacher walked past Marblo stopped what he was saying and seemed to gather himself '...oh ...well...erm...never mind' he seemed embarrassed. 'Ok, anyway, you'll find out ...follow me' he said confidently and strode off with the girls behind.

'That was odd' whispered Em. 'It was like he was going to say something and changed his mind.'

'Maybe he just forgot' Jade whispered back.

The girls hurried along behind Marblo. He stopped abruptly in front of a locker 'Here we are' he announced with another hand flourish and took a step back. Jade turned to thank Marblo but he appeared to have vanished! Em caught Jades eye and just shrugged.

'Ok Jade, get your stuff in the locker before we have to go to History' Em said consulting her map 'It's back in the new part of school so we can't be too long here'.

 Jade searched in her pockets for the key.

'Tissue, oh hang on...no mint!' Jade fumbled around.

'Hurry up or we are going to be late, the bell will go any minute' Em said looking at her watch.

'Oh ok, let's go then, I dare not be late to a lesson' Jade agreed 'I'll sort my locker out later', and the girls rushed off to their first lesson.

Jade still hadn't managed to unlock her locker, but at least she knew where it was.

Chapter 4

Em and Jade walked to lunch and joined the queue for a baguette.

'I just love these baguettes the barbeque chicken is just my favourite' Jade said as they sat down. 'I'm looking forward to Art after lunch, I've heard the teacher is really nice, I can't believe that we have already got 3 pieces of homework I'm going to have to get super organised', Jade chatted on not really realising that Em wasn't listening.

'I wonder where Marblo went' said Em quite out of the blue.

In between mouthfuls of baguette Jade replied 'I'm not sure, probably he just scooted round the corner and we didn't notice, I bet he's really busy and would have lots to do so he rushed off..... or he's magical and can teleport or something.' Em and Jade both laughed, but were thinking that maybe that could be true.

At the end of the day Jade was by herself as Em had decided to join the school choir and the first club meeting was that afternoon, Em had tried to persuade Jade to go too, 'Please you could just give it a go' Em had pleaded doing daft puppy dog eyes. Jade didn't really want to let her new best friend down but singing really wasn't her thing so she passed on that one. The girls agreed to meet the next morning just outside the gates so they could walk into school together.

Jade's bag was feeling extra heavy as they had been issued with text books today, so she decided to pop them in her locker, not wanting to lug them all the way home in one go 'I may as well make use of the locker' Jade thought.

Remembering the way Marblo had shown them earlier that day Jade meandered through the corridors to get to her locker. Lots of other children had the same idea and they were busy stuffing text books into their lockers. A couple of friends said 'Hi' to Jade as she passed, turning off the main corridor it was a lot quieter and walking down she had time to realise what a state it was in. Every other time she'd been down here it had been in a rush so she hadn't noticed. The pale grey paint was peeling off the walls revealing the original vibrant colours beneath. Lights were flickering just above her head and there were buzzing sounds from the radiators that were trying to keep the vast hallway warm . As Jade passed some old notice boards near her locker she noticed, in amongst some old newspaper clippings of 'A' Level results and sporting achievements, a small note on red paper that had been pinned right on the edge of the notice board, it caught her eye and she read the scrawly handwriting that looked suspiciously like Mr March's as she recognised from the marking in her book.

" Watch out! Locker Number 50 is Haunted"

She looked up and down the corridor there was no one about.

'That's silly' she muttered and went to take down the red paper but it had already fallen off the notice board just before her fingers reached it and was blowing down the corridor out of her reach. It tumbled and fell as if on the breeze, but there was no breeze!?! A shiver ran down Jade's back.

'Come on Jade' she said to herself 'this is just daft'. She took the small gold key out of her pocket and opened locker 50.

Chapter 5

Jade opened the door with a creak as the rusty hinges hadn't been used in a while but there it was an empty locker. One shelf just above head height and a hook on the door, it was a bit dusty but was completely normal. Jade felt herself breath out.

Jade got the heavy text books out of her bag and went to place them in the locker, it was then she noticed there was an inch of dust in the back corners. 'Eww' she said out loud and taking a tissue from her pocket bent down to dust of the bottom of the locker floor before she put her books in. As she dusted her finger caught on a rough edge, 'Ouch' she snatched her hand away and looked at the finger for damage, but something else caught her eye a small part at the corner of her locker was missing, she peered closer and instead of the wall which you would expect to see there was something that looked a lot like grass! She leaned nearer so she could get a much better look and there seemed to be what looked like an exotic plant! It had large crimson red petals the ends looked as if they had been dipped in orange paint, long green leaves.

moved as if they were snakes heading for the light. Wide eyed Jade dumped her text books in the locker, confused and slightly scared she shut the door with force. She held the door shut tight with one hand while her other, shaking from the surprise, locked the door.

Scooping up her now much lighter bag she stepped back 'I must be going crazy' Jade thought as she dashed down the corridor, her heart beating so fast she could feel it in her chest, like a wild animal throwing itself against the walls of a cage. She didn't stop running until she was home.

Chapter 6

Jade hadn't slept very well and had woken up early so she was at school waiting for Em to arrive for what seemed like hours. As arranged they met just outside the gates and as soon as Em stepped out of her mums car Jade rushed over to her. Jade explained all about the locker and what had happened her words tumbled out in fast jumbled sentences.

'Whoa, slow down' Em Said' her eyes wide with fascination 'this is crazy, I don't believe it, you are going to have to show me'

Jade replied 'Ok, I will.'

So, the girls hurried to Jade's locker, she fumbled for the key in her pocket. 'Are you ready?' asked Jade.

'Yes, show me' Em said.

Jade opened the locker very slowly and pointed to the corner. Em stared through the missing bit of locker as Jade had done yesterday.

'OMG, it looks like you have a jungle in your locker' Em turned and smiled 'that's amazing' Em's face lit up with excitement with not a hint of worry or fear.

Jade laughed 'Do you think it's a jungle?' she asked.

'Well what if you could put a camera on a long stick and poked it through the gap, you could see what's really inside then, that would be awesome' Em said.

'Well I don't have a camera or a long stick so that wont work!' Jade laughed.

BBBBRRIINNGG

The bell broke the conversation. 'We have to go' Jade closed the locker, 'Let's come back at the end of the day and we can investigate further' she suggested.

It's then they noticed Mr March coming around the corner, he stopped dead, looked at them and then glanced at Jades locker.

'Everything ok girls?' he asked.

'Yes Sir, we are just on our way to our next lesson' Em replied.

'Well quickly then, there's no need to be hanging around here.'

'Yes, Sir' they said and made their way to class.

Lessons seemed to take forever, and all the girls could talk about was locker 50, they had to speak in whispers so that no one overheard. Jade didn't feel scared anymore, having Em to share this with was brilliant.

Finally, the last bell of the day rung and they headed down the winding corridors to locker 50. Strangely, like yesterday there was no one around. Jade opened the locker door and knelt to look through the missing bit.

'Try and open up the hole a bit, so we can get a better look' said Em.

Jade gently tried pulling the corner that had fallen away but it was tricky the locker appeared to be made of some sort of metal and it hurt Jade's fingers as she pulled.

'Come on' Em moaned impatiently.

'It's tough, I don't see you helping!' Jade smiled up at her friend.

'Why don't you try and push instead?' Em suggested.

And so Jade did, with a good shove a large piece of the back of the locker fell and what she saw left her awestruck.

'Oh my!' gasped Jade.

Em appeared at her shoulder and peered through the hole.

'Now that's cool, lets explore' Em whispered.

What the girls could see was amazing.

Chapter 7

The girls were small enough to squeeze one by one into the locker and through the broken back into this strange but beautiful place. Jade couldn't believe she was standing with her best friend inside her locker, that was not really a locker, but a doorway to a magical jungle.

It was warm from the glowing sun but the air smelt damp as if there had been rain just a moment ago, they could see jungle plants and bright flowers in all colours imaginable. They could hear bird calls and the buzz of insects it was full of life but so peaceful.

All of a sudden a macaw flapped past and landed on a

 branch near the girls, cawing loudly it ruffled its feathers and seemed to be looking directly at them. 'Hello pretty bird' Jade said softly.

'You're not to bad yourself' the bird said back.

'That's funny,' said Em 'someone's taught him to say that' she laughed.

The bird seemed to roll his eyes and sit up straighter 'You humans can be so silly' he said 'Why would I need to be taught phrases? Well at least you can hear and understand me' he went on 'OK, well my name is Fisica, and most people can't pronounce it, you have to say Fizz-ee-ka, but you can call me Fizz for short ...and I suppose it's nice to meet you both' and he extended a wing as if expecting Em and Jade to shake it.

This is when it all became too much for Jade; the jungle seemed to spin before her eyes and she felt a wave of dizziness flow from her toes to her head, and she passed out!

While we are waiting for Jade to come round let me give you some more information about the locker jungle.

Just imagine this, tall trees in all shades of green stand proudly, vines twist from their branches to sweep the lush ground. Monkeys swing whooping to each other in a playful manner.

Dappled sunlight streams through the beautiful tree top canopy .Flowers of every colour and every scent bloom in drifts on the jungle floor. Butterflies with iridescent wings flit between the flowers, resting for just a moment before flying on in graceful arcs.

The smell of the air is fresh and out of sight a waterfall is crashing in the distance. And, of course, there is a talking parrot named Fisica, the parrot is ruby red, yellow and brilliant blue a most eye catching and majestic animal.

Chapter 8

When Jade cam too Em was staring right at her as she lay there in the school corridor, 'the jungle was all a dream' thought Jade as she felt the hard floor beneath her, and saw the familiar walls of the school around her. The strip light above her on the ceiling was buzzing and flickering a bit.

'How long have I been out cold for?' she asked Em.

'Ages, and I had to drag you out of the locker!' Em said ' You're not hurt, you just went all funny and fainted!' She smiled kindly at Jade.

Jade sat up 'So it wasn't a dream?' she asked Em.

'What? The Jungle? ...no way, that's all real....I think, it's very crazy, I can hardly believe it myself' Em said helping Jade to her feet.

'What time is it? my mum will be so worried that I'm not home' it suddenly occurred to Jade that school had finished hours ago.

'6.43 to be exact,' said Em checking her watch '..and don't worry I called your mum to say that you are at mine for a sleepover so she's collecting you at ten tomorrow morning'

'Wow' said Jade 'You are so organised!'

The girls crept down the corridor to find a way out of the school, they had everything crossed that they wouldn't set off an alarm or bump into any teachers that were working late. They remembered that in the girl's toilet block there was a window that never shut properly, so using the paper towel bin to balance on they wiggled and squeezed their way out of the window. Slipping through the hedge boundary of the school they were out. Both girls let out a massive breath of relief and ran to Em's house for the unplanned sleepover.

'Hi girls, nice to meet you Jade, please call me Sally' Em's mum welcomed them at the door and she seemed just as lovely as Em, she too had the blondest hair ever and a big smile, she was wearing blue jeans and stripy jumper, and holding oven gloves in one hand. The smell of cooking wafted out from the kitchen, she beamed at the girls.

'You two must be starving. I popped a pizza in the oven, its ready just about now!' She said making her way into the kitchen. 'Did you enjoy the afterschool club?' she called over her shoulder 'It finishes rather late I thought, in my day you'd be home for 5 at the latest.'

Em called 'Yes, it was, erm, interesting!' very loudly and quickly before Jade could say anything. The girls smiled sheepishly at each other.

Jade didn't realise quite how hungry she was until she sat down to eat the piping hot pepperoni pizza. They ate as quickly as they could without burning their mouths on the lovely melting cheese. They chatted about school to Em's mum, but really all they wanted to talk about was the fantastic jungle they had found.

'Thank you Sally, that was really tasty' Jade said as the girls finished off the food.

'You are welcome, here have some fruit and a biscuit' She said handing over the snacks ' Em why don't you take Jade to your bedroom, you two girls can have a chat about boys or makeup or whatever else is cool these days.'

'Muumm!' Em laughed rolling her eyes.

'This way' Em called to Jade as they made their way upstairs. Em's bedroom was a chalky shade of blue with a white metal framed bed that was situated right under the window. Her duvet cover had a pretty feather print all over in pastel shades. Em's carpet was one of those super fluffy ones that your toes just sink into, she had a big wardrobe and lots of shelves with knick-knacks on. A blow-up mattress was already set up for Jade to sleep on for the night, and it looked so welcoming.

'Your room is lovely' Jade told Em. They flopped down onto Em's bed, they were both quite tired after all the excitement of the day. As they chomped through the snacks that Em's mum had given them they looked up jungles and parrots on Em's phone until they finally felt too sleepy and started to doze off.

That night Jade dreamt about what she had seen, but in her dream the animals were chanting 'Save us, save us, save us'; she woke with a start, and glanced round at the unfamiliar bedroom.

Em was asleep in the bed next to her and she started talking in her sleep 'wow, pretty flowers and monkeys' she murmured. Jade smiled to herself Em was obviously dreaming about the jungle too.

Jade snuggled down and went back to sleep.

Chapter 9

In the morning the girls decided that they should tell an adult about the secrets of locker 50; so when Jade's mum picked her up she tried to explain the events of the last week. Unsurprisingly her mum didn't believe her.

'You have an over active imagination, I love it, you've always been good at telling stories' she said her eyes forward concentrating on driving. 'Oh, but talking about lockers I've had a letter from the school saying that they are refurbishing some old lockers, I think one of them might be yours....anyway you'll have to hand your key back and get a new one'

Jades jaw dropped 'Seriously?, but I don't want a new locker, mines just perfect.'

'Well Mr March said that's what's happening, so I'm afraid you'll just have to go along with it.'

'Did you say Mr March?'

'Yes, the letter came from him, I got it this morning like I said...don't worry you've still got a week of your old locker, but won't a nice new one be better?'

'No not really' Jade huffed.

Jade would have to try and prove her magical locker was real to her mum so that she could keep it, but she had no real evidence. Then she remembered that Em had her phone with her at school yesterday, may be she had some pictures.

The thing that was puzzling Jade was how Mr March kept popping up, he definitely seemed to dislike Jade and Em. He acted strangely when he found out she had Locker 50 and now he was the teacher trying to take it away from her due to 'refurbishment'.

When Jade got home she called Em immediately to ask her about the pictures and tell her about the letter from the school.

Em thought she was being daft about Mr March and that it was all just coincidence.

'But if I get a new locker we wont be able to visit the jungle again' pointed out Jade.

'Well we'll just have to make the most of it while we can.'

'Definitely' said Jade 'I promise not to faint again!'

It turned out that Em had taken some pictures, Jade just couldn't wait until Monday to see them. Not often did she wish her weekend away, but Monday just couldn't come around quickly enough.

Chapter 10

Jade woke early on Monday and left for school in a whirl of excitement. She met Em at the gate as usual. Em already had her phone out to show Jade the pictures. She had a couple of the jungle and some flowers and one of Fiscia. 'I'm not the best at taking photos, they've all come out a bit fuzzy' said Em.

'Never mind at least we have a few, that will prove to mum the jungle exists.'

'Let's go and see if it's still there, we have a bit of time before we need to go to our form class' Em said putting her phone in her pocket.

Of course it was still there, Jade and Em stepped through the locker and just stood there for a moment to take it all in. Fisica flew in to greet them, he landed near them on a branch that bent dramatically under his weight (he wasn't a particularly heavy bird he just picked a very flimsy branch to sit on, a bit like pigeons do!) Adjusting himself and finally balancing he said, without so much as a good morning. 'You've come back, that's good. Ok you need to find the Wise One to save the animals and the jungle, it's getting really bad!'

They looked surprised and a bit confused.

'Morning Fizz! Save them from what, what's getting really bad?' Em asked.

 'And where will we find the Wise One?' added Jade.

'So many questions' Fizz almost huffed 'The mean humans are taking the trees away and using them and the land for their own needs' stated Fizz ' Don't they understand the destruction?' he looked sad 'the Wise One knows what you must do, he can be found in the treetops.'

'Up there?' Jade pointed, her eyes rising to the jungle canopy 'but who is this Wise One, how will we know who to find?'

'They say he is the slowest in speed of them all, but he is so very fast in the mind, he is the most philosophical. He can hang around for days just thinking and eating' Fizz shuffled a bit more on his branch.

Jade stood there for a moment trying to figure out what animal it could possibly be. Monkeys hang around in trees and they are certainly very clever, but not slow. A tortoise is very slow so would have time to think but they would never be found hanging around in trees. Then PING suddenly it was obvious, what lives in trees and is very slow and has a lot of time to think and be philosophical, or should that be philo*sloth*ical, she smiled at her own joke.

'Is the Wise One a sloth by any chance?' asked Jade.

'Yes, you silly thing' Squawked Fizz. 'Of course he is.'

'Then why didn't you just tell us in the first place if you knew?' Em questioned.

'I had to check that you were clever enough to help....I didn't want a half brain human messing in the jungle! I mean you have the right colour eyes and everything.. .but still' Fizz flapped his wings 'come on then.'

WWWHHHHOOOSSSHHHH

The girls were suddenly balancing on the branch of a very tall tree high up in the jungle's canopy.

'Whoa how did we get up here?' the girls said in unison.

Then they heard a familiar sound a ringing bell, it sounded very far away and kind of muffled.

'That sounds like the school bell' Em said 'What shall we do?'

But before Jade could even think of an answer the branch of the tree gave way and the girls were tumbling down, the colours of the jungles rushing past vivid green, reds, yellows and blues all merged as they fell. They landed on the mossy jungle floor not with a thump, like they had expected, but much more gently quite like how a leaf falls from it's tree in Autumn. Again they heard the bell ring, this time it was much clearer. Dusting themselves down they squeezed through the locker and out into the school hallway.

'This is getting seriously weird' Em said as they grabbed their bags.

The morning lessons were really busy so it wasn't until lunchtime that Jade and Em had a chance to chat. The dinning hall was packed and there were no free tables.

The weather was still nice so the girls went outside and found a bench tucked away so they could talk without anyone else hearing.

'I'm still finding bits of moss in my hair' Jade laughed as she pulled yet another little green frond out.

'We need more time in the jungle' said Em.

'I Know' Jade agreed 'We will keep being interrupted by the bell, we need a lot more time, especially if we are expected to save the jungle, we can't just do that in 10 minutes.'

Em crunched away thoughtfully on her crisps.

'Maybe we could sneak in on Saturday?' Suggested Jade.

'I know it's a bit naughty, but the jungle obviously needs us for some reason, I can just sense that it's really important.'

Em thought this was the only solution, so they hatched a plan. They would just say that the school had an overnight camping trip, that way they could take supplies in case they needed anything whilst saving the jungle. The girls thought it was a perfect plan; although they did feel bad about the fibbing to their mums, but they knew it was all for the good of the jungle and they would explain everything in the end and they were sure their mums would understand.

Chapter 11

It was Saturday and the plan was in action, Jade had packed a small backpack full of useful things for the 'camping trip' she hugged her mum goodbye and headed off to school. She had arranged to meet Em outside the school gates. Em had got there earlier and had been trying to find a way in. She greeted Jade looking worried.

' I'm sorry I had a good look but I can't seem to find a way in' Em said 'the toilet window must have been fixed, I couldn't opened it however hard I tried.'

'We can't fail, we have to have another look, we can't just give up' said Jade.

The girls slipped through the hedge as they had done the other day and went around to the playground. They ran to the older part of the school where the locker was, there were lots of windows but all seemed to be shut tight. It was then they heard someone humming a tune.

'Oh no' someone is here' said Jade.

Jade turned around and there was Marblo 'Girls you're not supposed to be here' he said in a firm voice but with a twinkle in his eyes 'You better come in now!' he winked at them. As if to mean don't worry.

The girls followed Marblo into the school 'Wait here girls' he said ' I shall be back with you in a moment.'

'Do you think he's going to call our parents?' whispered Em, she looked worried. 'We'll be in so much trouble.'

'I don't think so, don't ask me why but I think he knows why we are here' Jade replied 'and I think he wants to help.'

Marblo reappeared holding a bright red tail feather from a parrot of some sort. Jade instantly thought of Fizz's brightly coloured feathers.

'Here, you might need this, it's my last one so use it wisely!' Marblo said and handed Jade the feather. 'Off you go then girls.' With a little sigh he then started to hum and sweep the floor once more making his way down the corridor away from the girls.

'Let's go then' said Jade.

Em was looking a bit dazed 'You were right, he just seems to want to help us', with that Jade and Em scurried off to Jade's locker.

The corridor was, of course, empty but the girls had a funny feeling that they were being watched. Jade could sense that Em was nervous, her normal easy smile was replaced by a more serious look.

'It's going to be ok' said Jade as she slid the little gold key in the lock. The door opened easily and the girls squeezed through the back panel one by one as they had done before.

'It still takes my breath away' said Jade ' every time I'm here I can't help but think how beautiful this jungle is, it makes me sad to think it's in danger.'

'That's why we need to help' said Em 'It seems very peaceful today with no squawking from Fizz.'

'Yes, I wonder where that funny parrot is' said Jade starting to walk further into the jungle. 'How are we going to get to the treetops to find the Wise One without Fizz?', worried Jade.

'I suppose we could make a sort of ladder, or climb?' Suggested Em as she stepped up onto a moss covered boulder.

It's then Jade remembered the feather that Marblo had given them and what he had said. She pulled the feather out of her pocket telling Em 'I think this is why Marblo wanted us to have this.'

'But what use is a single feather' Em said grabbing it and waving it around, then suddenly within a hundredth of a second the girls were once again in the treetops.

Steadying themselves on the broadest branch they could find the girls looked around. 'Well I think that single feather was quite useful' smiled Jade. The girls sensed they were not alone.

'Hello there' came a very slow, low voice. Looking up to the branch above them they saw a sloth, they had found 'The Wise One', or had he found them it was hard to tell. He moved slowly closer and appeared to be studying them with great concentration, his coat was grey with patches of something green that looked very much like moss, he really was very well camouflaged against his leafy backdrop, except for the red bow tie he was wearing?!

'Hello! We were told to find you to save the jungle, but we are not sure how' the girls explained in unison.

The Wise Ones eye glistened as he explained 'In the South West people are cutting all the trees down, it's destroying our beautiful jungle. They are using machines that we can't fight or reason with. We needed some 'chosen' humans to help as the tree cutters don't understand us. You two girls have been chosen' he finished.

'Why us? Why are we the chosen humans?' asked Jade.

' Ahh ' The Wise One said, 'The jungle gods said we needed to find two young and bright minds, that belonged to brave and curious people. Before we have been guarded by one chosen one, but alas he is now too old and as the destruction has become worse we need two ...not one... do you understand?' he yawned before carrying on 'and the key thing was that they have to be best friends and both have bright green eyes like the jungle trees you see' he said pointing at the vivid colour of the tree canopy.

The girls looked at each other, and tried to take in all the new information. They did both have very bright green eyes, they were young and certainly curious, otherwise they wouldn't be there. How brave they were was yet to be tested, but they were best friends.

'But how are we going to get to them and stop the machines?' the girls asked looking intently at the sloth.

'They need power for the machines, the power has to be changed, and once this happens the destruction will stop' the sloth said simply and yawned once more 'if you need to get help and need to get to me just say 'I'm feeling philoslothical' .... ok?'

'Good luck girls' he said scratching his head 'remember, the more you know the more you know you don't know....I'll send you right there'.

Chapter 12

Before the girls could even ask the sloth how they'd get there (wherever 'there' was!) they found themselves crouched behind a bush, all around them was destruction, tree stumps everywhere, logs in huge piles, men in enormous machines, with **'March Industries'** stamped boldly across the sides rumbled past them making the ground shake and filling the air with fumes and noise. They were horrified, this was so different from the beautiful jungle they loved.

Jade had a look of determination on her face 'I'm going to sort this out!'

'What's the plan?' Em asked.

'I'm not 100% sure but the Wise One said we need to change the power so I guess he means switch it off, what do you think?' Jade asked.

'I suppose you could be right, but how would switching the power stop the destruction forever?' questioned Em

Jade shrugged and both the girls crouched lower as a truck rumbled past shaking the ground so much they could see tiny rocks dancing on the ground surface. They ducked lower behind the bush.

'Right, I'll go and see what I can do, I'll try and find the main power source and shut it off.'

'Ok' said Em 'I will wait here, and raise the alarm if I see any danger heading your way' she looked very worried, 'I'll get help if I don't see you in 10 minutes, ok?'

'Ok' Jade gave her best friend a hug and took a deep breath.

She dodged between tree stumps crouching low as men and vehicles passed by her, she didn't want to be spotted. Jade made her way further into the destruction, her heart ached for what she could see, this was just so wrong. A massive truck growled past causing a great dust cloud to rise, Jade rubbed her eyes that felt as though they were now full of grit. As the cloud of dust settled she spotted a wooden building not too far away, 'there has to be something in there' she thought. Crouching behind a tree stump she watched the building carefully, a couple of men came out and got in a digger and drove passed her hiding place. She stayed and waited a little longer just to make sure everyone had gone.

'Come on, be brave' she thought as she dashed across open land to the door of the wooden building.

The door swung open easily and inside was a complete mess, there was a desk covered in paperwork and coffee cups and there were all sorts of plans and maps pinned to the walls. There were work jackets hanging on a row of pegs and printed on the back was **March Industries**. There was one window and on the window sill were some plants that all appeared to be dead and gathering dust..... 'oh my goodness' Jade said aloud it was at that moment Jade made the connection.

March Industries had to be run by Mr March, that was why he was acting so strangely and didn't want Jade to have locker 50. He must have known she'd find out what he was up to.

Jade moved over to the desk and looked at the paperwork, she shuffled through the piles of papers not really knowing what she was looking for and it was then Jade found something terrible.

She held up the plan in disbelief, her eyes filled with tears, the plan was to make a museum of stuffed animals that have been killed whilst cutting down the trees. This was getting worse and worse, she stuffed the plan angrily into her pocket.

'There is no time to lose' Jade thought, 'I must cut off the power'. Leaving the messy desk she starting scanning around the office again then she noticed a big button encased in glass it looked a bit like the ones you see in the movies, but instead of Do Not Touch written above it, it said POWER.

Bingo!

Lifting the dusty glass case lid carefully, Jade took a deep breath and pushed the button hard.

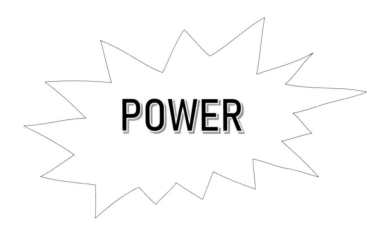

POWER

For a moment nothing happened and then with a final lurch and pop everything was silent.

So silent in fact that Jade could hear her own heart beating.

Voices of angry men started shouting and she could hear footsteps coming, Jade had no time to sneak out slowly, so she just ran and ran back to where Em was hiding, her heart was beating so hard and her feet pounded the ground.

Chapter 13

Em sprang up from her hiding place 'You did it!' Em exclaimed 'Well done' she jumped up and down on the spot.

'Come on they've seen us' Jade panted 'and they don't look very happy!'

They ran as fast as they could swerving and dodging out of eyeshot. Huffing and puffing they took cover behind a huge pile of logs.

'What was it like in there?' Em asked when she got her breath back.

'It was messy, horrible, absolutely terrible, but at least I found the power button. I was so worried I'd be caught. You'll never guess what, but I think March Industries is run by Mr March!.' Jade added.

'Mr March, as in our English teacher?' Em looked momentarily confused as she considered what Jade had told her 'Hey you could be right, it totally makes sense , that's why he was acting so weird'

'And what's worse there were all these horrible plans lying around' Jade started to explain the plans she had found, and in particular the plan that was crumpled up and stuffed in her pocket. Em listened, her jaw dropped, and her eyes were wide.

It was then the girls heard rumbling of machinery starting up.

'I don't understand it, I definitely switched the power off' Jade looked confused 'The machinery stopped, I stopped the power just like we were told to do!'

'Come on Jade, I think we need some more help!' Em exclaimed grabbing her friends hand.

They started to run from their hiding place away towards the green vibrant jungle they knew, then Jade remembered what the sloth had said.

'Say the words' she panted to Em.

'What words?'

'The ones the sloth said, if we needed help' their bright green eyes twinkled.

'Ready, 1...2...3 'I'm feeling philo*slothi*cal' they shouted together.

POOF there they were, standing right next to the sloth 'You needed me?' he asked.

'Well, Jade was so awesome, I only really hid! But Jade was brilliant she found the button and shut down the power' Em blurted out.

'So, you don't need me, the jungle is saved?' the Wise One asked.

'No, we do need you, you see the men just turned the power back on, we don't understand' Jade said 'You said we needed to change the power and we did, but it didn't work'

The sloth looked at Jade carefully he nodded slowly 'I said the power source must change to stop the destruction, you simply turned off the power for the machines'

'Why don't you just tell us what we need to do' Jade was starting to feel cross with the Wise One. 'Oh, and I also found this' Jade pulled the crumpled plans out of her pocket and handed them to the sloths outstretched arm. He took the paper and studied it carefully.

'Well I never!, this was worse than I could have imagined' he seemed flabbergasted.

'What are we going to do?' asked Jade.

The wise one looked slowly and carefully at the girls and popped the plans in his mouth!

The girls looked at each other in confusion. Was he actually going to eat them? It took him a long, long while to chew through the paper. Em and Jade didn't know what to do, so they just stood and watched both trying not to giggle, it was like watching the worlds slowest paper shredder in action. It was quite ridiculous.

Finally, with a huge gulp and a hiccup the Wise One said 'Well that's that sorted', he scratched his head. 'Now you two just need to work out how to stop destruction, find out what the power is behind March Industries and stop that' he started to turn away from them and made his way back to the cover of the treetops.

'He makes it sound so simple but so complicated all in one ' Em said to Jade. 'What should we do....eat the machines like he ate the paper?' Em snorted.

'I must say he's not being very helpful.'

'Talking of eating, I'm starving I think we need a break and a think' Em said sensibly 'What's in that backpack, have you got any food?'

'Yes lots.'

Jade and Em sat down on a low branch that looked out over the beautiful jungle. They ate near enough all the snacks that Jade had packed. All the while they were thinking of what the Wise One had said and just how they were going to save the jungle.

Chapter 14

'I think we need some more advice' said Jade 'and I don't think the Wise One is going to give us anymore help!'

The girls pondered.

'Who else knows about the jungle and can help us? You said your mum didn't believe you so why should anyone else?'

Em thought for a moment longer.

'You know how Marblo helped us, do you think he might be able to help again?' Em asked.

'Good call, it's definitely worth a try, after all he gave us the feather and do you remember when he said I was the perfect person to look after locker 50? It's like he already knew it was special.'

'Ok, let's see if he's still in school, it's got to be worth a try.'

The girls clambered down from the branch and made their way back through the locker, they didn't have to search far as Marblo was just outside in the corridor.

He spoke first 'It's quite some locker, eh?'

Jade smiled at him nodding 'You know what's inside don't you?'

Marblo smiled 'I know it very well, I was a pupil here too and this was my locker, I used to visit the jungle often and help when I could. Is Fisica still around?' Jade nodded, Marblo smiled and continued 'I used to be able to talk to the animals but my mind became too old and now I don't hear them anymore. I don't suppose The Wise One still wears that silly old bow tie I gave him?'

'Yes!' the girls laughed 'We wondered how he got that!'

'He's a fascinating chap' said Marblo 'He thought it made him look even more intellectual.'

Marblo stopped talking and look carefully at the girls 'Something's wrong isn't it?'

'Yes, we need your help, something is very wrong.'

Jade went on to explain to Marblo about the destruction, and how they thought they'd stopped the power and of what the Wise One had said (and done with the awful plans!) Marblo listened carefully to all they had to say.

'....and the thing is we think that Mr March is behind it all' finished Jade.

Marblo didn't seem to look surprised, instead he shook his head 'Oh dear, I had thought something was up, the jungle has been happy and peaceful for a long time. But just at the start of this school year I thought I heard a call for help from Fisica' he paused 'and I fear you may be right about Mr March he was the only new teacher this September and his office backs on to the same wall as your locker does, Jade, so he may have found a way into the jungle.'

'So, you think this is all down to him?' Em gasped.

'I'm afraid it looks that way.'

'Well we need to stop him, maybe that's what the Wise One meant .... Mr March is the power that needs to be changed'

Chapter 15

The girls knew they had to change Mr March's heart, a little like they do in fairy tales, they needed him to see what he was doing was bad and get him to stop. However, unlike a fairy tale they didn't have a magic wand or a secret potion to help them, they only had what they knew, and what they knew was that the beautiful jungle was being destroyed needlessly.

'Ok' said Jade firmly 'we need to find Mr March and show him just how wonderful this jungle is and persuade him to change his ways and stop trying to cut it down.'

'I agree, and I will help all I can' said Marblo 'let me just fetch something, I'll be back in a moment.'

'Do you think we are going to be able to do this?' Em asked.

'Well, we are going to have to try before it's too late' Jade stated confidently.

Marblo reappeared carrying what looked like a photo album 'Ok girls, I think we should wait in Mr March's office, he'll have to come out sooner or later.'

As they entered the office Jade remember the last time she was there for her detention and she felt a shiver run down her spine. The same dead plants were on the windowsill collect yet more dust it was clear to see that Mr March certainly didn't seem to like nature at all.

'So, is that the door he came out of?' asked Em pointed to back of the office.

'Yep' nodded Jade 'So I guess we just wait?'

But it seemed silly, the three of them just hanging around an empty office.

'Let me just check in that cupboard' Marblo said 'After all, no one can tell me off, if I'm just cleaning it!' he winked.

It wasn't long before Marblo reappeared he was holding a large notebook that had a leather cover with gold lettering on.

'I found this' he said holding it out 'it may explain why Mr March is so keen to cut down the jungle.'

They opened the note pad and read through just the first few pages. It seemed to be some kind of instruction book written in old fashioned handwriting.

'Look at this part' said Marblo pointing and reading aloud... ' *to find the treasure you deserve you must seek Emerald and Jade, you will find them in a secret jungle, then your heart will be rich.....*'

'And what do we have here?' came a low growl of a voice that made the girls jump.

Mr March loomed next to them glaring at the book that Marblo was holding.

'Oh, I was just cleaning your cupboard for you and I found a book that looks rather interesting," Marblo said.

'Well you shouldn't be snooping around my stuff, and what are these students doing here?' Mr March hissed through gritted teeth.

Marblo looked lost for words so Jade decided it was time to be brave.

'Mr March, we know what you are doing, you must stop destroying the jungle, it's just not fair to destroy such a beautiful thing.'

'Huh, it *will* be beautiful when I can start the mining for the gems, that's what you two were up to snooping around trying to find the treasure.'

'Gems, what gems?' asked Em confused.

'And we certainly weren't trying to find any treasure' added Jade.

'You've seen the book, Marblo was reading it when I came in' he snatched the book from Marblo 'here it says in black and white that I will find Jade and Emeralds in the jungle and then I'll be rich!'

'But Sir, I'm not sure that's what it means' Jade said confidently.

'Rubbish, what else could it possibly mean?'

Jade and Em glanced at each other smiling, at that moment they both knew what it meant, it was obvious really.

'I think' started Em 'that the book is saying you have to find Jade and myself in the jungle, you see my real name is Emerald I was named after the colour of my eyes, I just shorten it to Em.'

Mr March looked puzzled, but the angry look was gone.

'But how will finding you make me rich?'

'It's your heart that will become rich, I don't think it's talking about money.'

'Please Sir, come with us' Jade asked hopefully.

Mr March seemed to soften he looked at Marblo who nodded.

'Come through locker 50 and see what a beautiful place the jungle is.'

Slightly reluctantly Mr March agreed, the four of them squeezed through the back of the locker and out into the jungle. Em and Jade had become quite familiar with this place and led the way through the large trees with the twisted vines and out onto a little clearing where you could see for miles over the lush green jungle. Mr March had been very quiet, he just stood there gazing out. 'I've been destroying all this?' he asked.

'Yes, Sir' the girls said in unison.

'And there are no gems?'

'No Sir, just us!' they laughed.

Marblo stepped forward 'Look Mr March' he said holding out the photo album he collected earlier 'these are the pictures from the arboretum that I used to look after, people would come from miles just to see the beautiful plants, people really do care.'

Mr March studied the photos 'I think people would come from miles away to see this jungle' Suddenly Mr March seemed to change like a light had been switched on, his smile seemed natural and his dark eyes seemed warm.

'I'm going to stop the destruction, I'll tell my workmen to stop cutting down the trees' he stated, the girls were so thrilled they hugged each other hard.

'I think everyone should be able to appreciate all this' he said 'I should open it up for the public to come and see, I could make a lot of money on the entrance fee.'

'NOOOOO' Jade and Em said together 'The jungle isn't a tourist attraction, we just need to look after it and care for it'.

'Ok!' said Mr March smiling 'You girls win, we'll look after this jungle.'

Mr March lent up against a tree 'I think I'll stay here for a while longer, if that's ok?'

Jade and Em smiled at each other, they really had changed his heart. At that moment there was a rustling up above and The Wise One made a very slow entrance.

'Jade, Em' he called 'Thank you girls, you have saved this paradise, no more trees will fall now, thanks to you two. Make sure you come and visit whenever you want to' and with that he slowly turned around and made his way back into the jungle.

The End….well, for now anyway.

About Me

When I finished writing 'Jade' I was 11 years old, but whilst this was my first book it certainly wasn't my first story. Since starting Primary School I would fill note books with stories and present them proudly to my class teachers, their kind words of encouragement made me want to write more and more.

I love reading, writing, being creative and of course watching daft videos on my phone! I train weekly to compete in 'Equestrian Vaulting' and I love to ride my fabulous pony.

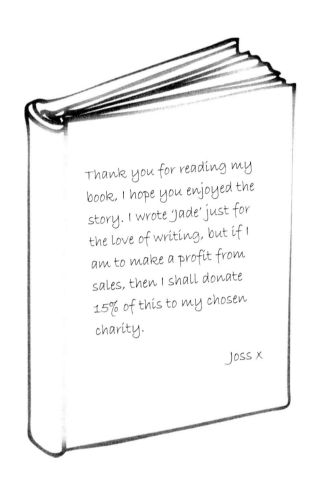

Thank you for reading my book, I hope you enjoyed the story. I wrote 'Jade' just for the love of writing, but if I am to make a profit from sales, then I shall donate 15% of this to my chosen charity.

Joss X

Jade's Jungle Word Search

A	M	O	N	K	E	Y	F	P
P	E	M	S	L	I	N	I	A
J	G	R	E	E	N	O	S	R
B	U	W	A	D	E	L	F	R
F	U	V	I	N	E	O	J	O
I	D	T	A	S	T	F	A	T
S	L	O	T	H	E	Y	D	E
R	A	P	F	E	I	O	E	S
H	E	W	O	L	R	F	N	S
S	R	E	W	O	L	F	P	E
U	A	C	I	S	I	F	L	E
L	B	Y	P	E	E	R	T	Y

Jade	Em		Parrot	Tree
Butterfly	Vine		Flower	Lush
Monkey	Green	Wise One	Fisica	Sloth

79